I0670739

Revolutionary Brain

GUIDE DOG BOOKS

Revolutionary Brain © 2012
by Harold Jaffe

Published by Guide Dog Books
Bowie, MD

First Edition

Cover Image: Matthew Revert
Book Design: Jennifer Barnes

Printed in the United States of America

ISBN: 978-1-935738-32-9

Library of Congress Control Number: 2012953442

www.GuideDogBooks.com

Revolutionary Brain

Essays & Quasi-Essays

by Harold Jaffe

Books by Harold Jaffe

Non-Fiction
Revolutionary Brain: Essays & Quasi-Essays
Beyond the Techno-Cave: A Guerrilla Writer's Guide to Post-Millennial Culture

Docufictions
OD
Paris 60
Terror-Dot-Gov
15 Serial Killers
False Positive

Novels
Jesus Coyote
Othello Blues
Dos Indios
Mole's Pity

Fiction Collections
Anti-Twitter: 150 50-Word Stories
Sex for the Millennium
Straight Razor
Eros Anti-Eros
Madonna & Other Spectacles
Beasts
Mourning Crazy Horse

Acknowledgments

Several of these texts were published in *American Book Review*, *Beuyscouts of America*, *New Border, Fiction International, Mad Hatters' Review, Boulevard, Electronic Book Review*, *Journal of Experimental Fiction, Map Literary*, *WIPS: Works (of Fiction) in Progress*, *Nuevo* (Madrid), *Le Pivot* (Paris).

Gratitude to Gary Lain for reading this volume in manuscript.

Contents

as abject, so the sacred

—Kristeva

Death in Texas

Date of Execution: March 3, 2004
Offender: Marcus Cotton #999252
County: Cherokee
Last Statement:

Well Moms, sometime it works out like this.

Love life, live long.

When you dealin' wit' reality, real ain' always what you wan' it to be.

Take care yousefs.

Tell my kids I love 'em.

God is real. He is fixin' to find out some deep things that are real.

Bounce back, baby, you know what I'm sayin'.

Yawl take care yousefs.

That's it, Warden.

Date of Execution: July 28, 2005
Offender: Virgil Ravenfeather #921338
County: Navarro
Last Statement:
Only the sky and the green grass goes on forever and today is a good day to die.

Date of Execution: January 16, 2002
Offender: Horace Allen #987225
County: Liberty
Last Statement:
Members of Mrs. Lackey's family, like I said, I take responsibility for the death of your daughter in 1989.

I'm deeply sorry for the loss of your beloved daughter.

I am a human being also, I know how it feels.

I cannot explain and can't give you no answers.

I can give you just one thing.

I'm'a give a life for a life.

I am not saying this to be facetious.

I hope yawl find comfort in my execution.

As for me, I am happy, that is why you see me smiling.

I am glad to be leaving this world.

I am going to a better place.

I have made peace with God, I am born again.

I hope you get over any malice or hatred you feel.

God bless all yawl.

[Sings]

Amazing Grace, how sweet the sound,

That saved a wretch like me,

I once was lost but now am found,

Was blind, but now, I see…

Date of Execution: February 8, 2003
Offender: Octavio Guerra #978923
County: Zapata
Last Statement:

I want to thank my family for their help and moral support and their struggle. Woulda been a whole lot harder without their love.

Me? I'm just going back home. I will see yawl one of these days.

Just don't rush it. I will be there always. I'll be watching over you.

I love yawl, huh.

I'll see yawl in Slayton, Texas.

Dios te mandas contigo mi espiritu.

Cuida mi familia.

Pull the plug, Warden.

Date of Execution: June 6, 2006
Offender: Timothy Tilton #906823
County: Red River
Last Statement:

I know you folks is here to find closure for the things I have done.

There are no words to describe the pain and suffering you have went through all these years, and that is something that I cannot take back from you.

I hope that Megan, if she is here present today, knows that today I hope you all get peace and joy.

I am sorry it has taken 14 years to get closure.

If it would have brung closure or brung her back, I would have did this years ago.

I promise, I promise.

I didn't mean to inflict the pain and suffering on your family.

I pray that she is safe in heaven.

I pray that you find closure and strength.

I am sorry, I am truly sorry.

You all take care.

Pastor, tell Megan I am sorry.

Date of Execution: June 13, 2001
Offender: Johnny Saginaw #999222
County: San Jacinto
Last Statement:
I regret what happened.

I did not harm no one.

Po' man he ain' nuffin' but shit on your bootsole.

Go 'head, do me.

Date of Execution: May 24, 2006
Offender: Jesus Aguilar #911383

County: Gillespie
Last Statement:
I would like to say to my family, I am alright.

> Leo? Donde esta, Leo?
>
> Esta aqui, Leo?
>
> Don't lie, man. Be happy.
>
> Are you happy?
>
> Are you all happy?

Date of Execution: September 27, 2004
Offender: Dwayne-Earl Clapp #999150
County: Scurry
Last Statement:
Sharla, Lamar, Sonny, Michelle, yawl know I love you.

Tell ever'body I said hey, I love 'em and I will see 'em on the other side. K?

Now I just pray that if there is anything 'gainst me—that God will take it on home.

I don't want nobody talkin' bad at nobody.

I don't want nobody bein' bitter.

Keep clean hearts and I will see yawl on the other side. K?

I love yawl, stay sweet.

Kick the tires and light the fire, I am goin' home to see my infant baby girl and my mom.

Date of Execution: August 14, 2002
Offender: Javier Suarez #944906

County: Palo Pinto

Last Statement:

First of all, I would like to apologize to the family members of the Cadena family for whatever hurt and suffering I caused you.

I hope you find it in your heart to forgive me.

The peace you find will be a temporary peace, true peace will come only through Jesus Christ.

I pray through this execution that you will find the peace you seek.

Give yourself to Jesus.

I thought about your loved one a whole lot.

He will be in heaven waitin' on me.

I will then talk to him personal and ask for his forgiveness.

To my family, I thank you and love you for being there for me and supporting me.

Forgive me for the pain I caused you.

[*Spanish*]

To all the people of Méjico that supported me: I carry each and every one of you in my heart.

If you are going to demonstrate, I don't want you to do nothing crazy to these people.

They are good people, they have suffered enough.

Long live Méjico.

Date of Execution: May 28, 2002
Offender: Napoleon Beazley III #999141
County: Rockwall

Last Statement:

The act I committed to put me here was brutal and senseless.

But the person that committed that act is no longer here—I am.

I'm not going to struggle physically against these restraints.

I'm not going to shout, use profanity or make threats.

Understand though that I am saddened by what is happening here tonight.

I'm disappointed that a system supposed to protect and uphold what is just can be so much like me when I made the same shameful mistake.

I'm sorry that John Luttig died.

And I'm sorry that it was something in me that caused all of this to happen to begin with.

Tonight we tell the world that there are no second chances in the eyes of justice.

Tonight we tell our children that in some instances killing is righteous.

There are a lot of men like me on death row—good men—who fell to the same misguided emotions.

Give those men a chance to do what's right, undo their wrongs.

A lot of them want to fix the mess they started, but don't know how.

The problem is the system is telling them there is no rehabilitation.

Only unforgiving punishment.

Date of Execution: September 11, 2001
Offender: Karla Faye Tucker #922923
County: Yuma
Last Statement:

I would like to say to the Mosebys that I am very, very sorry of depriving you of your mama and daddy.

To Warden Taggett and Chaplain Jesse Turner, I thank you very, very much, you been so good to me.

To my family and friends that has stuck by me, I love yawl from the bottom of my heart.

I am going to be face to face with Jesus now.

I will see all yawl when you get up there.

I will be dressed in wat.

Date of Execution: December 7, 2000
Offender: Claude Jones #980890
County: Nueces
Last Statement:

To your family, ah, I hope this can bring some closure to yawl.

I am sorry for your loss and, hey, I love all yawl.

Let's go.

Date of Execution: May 17, 2006
Offender: Jermaine Herron #979210
County: Potter
Last Statement:

Mr. Jerry Nutt, I just hope this brings some kind of peace to your family.

I wish I could bring them back, but I cain't.

I hope my death brings peace to you all.

Don't hang on to the hate.

Mama, I love you.

Lord forgive me for my sins because here I come.

Date of Execution: May 28, 2002
Offender: Adolf Wölfli #999666
County: San Augustine
Last Statement:
You gentlemen and ladies of quality who frequently don't know yourselves what Christian virtue and justice are, look at the sunken, deep-set eyes of the lower classes, where you can see all too clearly the sorrow and misery that weigh on their hearts.

Not everyone who sees his grieved and martyred face in the washroom mirror in the morning is a murderer or drug addict.

On the contrary, the grounds for his misery are to be sought elsewhere.

You friends near and far.

If among you there is anyone without sin, let him come to me, and I will implore him for compassion and mercy.

Date of Execution: April 20, 2005
Offender: Troy Kunkle #954811
County: Angelina

Last Statement:

I've been hanging around this popsicle stand way too long.

Before I leave, I want to tell you all.

Bury me deep, lay two speakers at my feet, put headphones on my skull and rock and roll me when I'm dead.

I'll see you all in hell.

Date of Execution: August 23, 2005
Offender: Jimmy Blackmon #924591
County: Hunt
Last Statement:

(This offender declined to make a final statement.)

Crisis Art

This guitar kills fascists
—Woody Guthrie

On September 5, 1981, the Welsh group that called itself "Women for Life on Earth" arrived on Greenham Common, in Berkshire, England. They had marched from Cardiff, Wales, with the intention of challenging the decision to site 96 US Cruise nuclear missiles on Greenham Common. On arrival they delivered a letter to the Base Commander that said: "We fear for the future of all our children and for the future of the living world."

When their request for a debate was ignored they set up a "Peace Camp" just outside the fence surrounding the Royal Air Force Greenham Common Airbase. This surprised the authorities and set the tone for an audacious, lengthy protest that was to last 19 years.

The protesters refused to allow authorities to enter the camp, which became known as the Women's Peace Camp and gained international recognition with imaginative images such as eggs, spider webs and children's toys with which they decorated the chain link fences and contested area. In the end the UK and US withdrew their attempt to site the cruise missiles in Greenham Common.

*

During the Augusto Pinochet dictatorship, a number of Chilean working-class women created complex tapestries depicting the harsh conditions of life and the pain resulting from the disappeared victims of Pinochet's repression. These tapestries, or arpilleras, get their name from the Spanish word for the burlap backing they used.

Working quietly and using traditional methods, the women's arpilleras came to have a wide influence within Chile and internationally. The tapestries preserved the memory of los desaparecidos and the dictatorship's brutality, as well as the unemployment, food shortages, housing shortages, and other hardships of daily life attributed to Pinochet's rule. Preserving this collective memory was itself an act of art-as-protest, but creating the arpilleras also empowered the women, many of whom experienced a liberation through their work and became involved in further protests against Pinochet's regime.

*

Krzysztof Wodiczko, born in Poland, emigrated to Canada, and currently lives in the US. He is particularly well-known for his guerrilla projections on official buildings purported to embody public values. Guerrilla, because his images were subversive and often projected without official permission. He sought, he explained, to unmask the buildings' existing rhetoric.

One of his first projections was a swastika on the façade of the South African embassy in London during Apartheid to implicate the British government and align them with the white Apartheid regime in South Africa. And to implicate the public building itself, which presented itself as an architectural emblem of moral value.

Later, during Ronald Reagan's presidency, Wodiczko created a two-part projection in San Diego and Tijuana addressing the links between illegal immigration into the US and California's economy, in which migrant labor plays a crucial role.

One projection is on the façade of a Spanish style building in San Diego's Balboa Park, called the Museum of Man, which professes to be an anthropologically egalitarian repository of art and artisanry, but which Wodiczko sees as a muted celebration of western colonialism.

His projected image aligns a pair of white, male, well-groomed hands impatiently clasped, as if waiting for his meal. Above and to the right are two coarse outstretched hands—manacled at the wrists—but holding an ample basket of fruit, and, imprisoned as they are, ready to serve their colonialist master.

*

Rirkrit Tirivanija is a Thai artist. One of his installations consisted of the following: He bicycled around looking for space: empty warehouse or aircraft hangar, deserted K-Mart, abandoned Rite-Aid, haunted Burger King.

He rented the space and furnished it with stoves, cooking gas, freezers, fridges, microwaves, counters, bowls, cups, glasses, plastic cutlery, chopsticks, Tupperware, folding tables, chairs.

He purchased food: noodles, rice, potatoes, bread, soup, salad, tofu, fruit, green tea, bottled water, cocoa, curry spices. Comfort food.

He engaged the homeless as helpers.

Food prepared, he invited the homeless helpers along with the lined-up homeless to eat.

Continued through the day, into the night. Clean up, close for the night. Sleep on the premises.

Do the same thing for 60 days.

After 60 days he closed the space, got on his bicycle and looked for another empty warehouse or aircraft hangar, terrorized Rite-Aid, spooked McDonald's, gutted Gap, bombed-out Home Depot.

Select the space, rent it.

Feed the homeless for 60 days.

Close up, move on, find another space, repeat.

*

The preceding represents four examples of creating art in times of conflict. In every instance the art is problematic; not esthetic, as such; not even palpable in the instance of Tirivanija feeding the homeless.

What is the difference between art as it is usually constructed and what might be called crisis art, or cultural activism: the use of cultural means to effect social change or a wider social awareness?

Art that responds to a crisis is situational, hence created rapidly rather than painstakingly revised and refined.

Crisis art is directed rather than disinterested; more closely related to art as process than product.

Crisis art is keenly aware of text and context.

Crisis art often works best collaboratively.

Collaboration contests the auratic view of the artist. "Auratic," coined by Walter Benjamin, refers to the artificial elevation of the artist to a position above his or her fellows.

Crisis art is "immoral."

Georges Bataille insisted that the strongest art must function as an "immoral subversion of the existing order"; because "morality" is in the possession of the existing order, and as such is never what it professes to be.

Crisis art is (to quote a still fashionable term coined by the Russian critic Bakhtin), "dialogic."

The idea is not that the artist stands above the fray paring his fingernails, bemusedly observing his creations. Dialogic articulates the more humbling notion that the artist interacts, even integrates, with the community, on a largely equal basis, each affecting and affected.

Crisis artists must swallow the poison in order to reconstitute it. Expel it art.

The poison, currently, includes our crazily spinning, electronic-obsessed, war-making culture and its profit-mad institutions; along with the rapidly worsening environmental crisis. The image of swallowing the poison and expelling it as art is shamanic.

But can art actually have any appreciable impact on the lives of humans who are oppressed, disenfranchised, struggling merely to survive? Can art affect cynical politicians and their corporate brethren?

There are precedents which were successful against great odds: Upton Sinclair's *The Jungle*; anti-slavery writings during the abolitionist period; French writers and artists helping to end the colonial war in Algeria; Solzhenitsyn's denunciation of Stalinism and the Gulags; Act-Up's culturally activist response to the demonizing of gay men during the AIDS crisis in the 80s and early 90s.

Do the kinds of strategies and calculations necessary for making and employing crisis art stand in opposition to the notion of the artist as dreamer, as creating from the deepest levels of consciousness?

Consider Goya, Blake and the French Revolution, the Mexican muralists, Grosz and Heartfield, Brecht, Picasso's Guernica, B Traven, John Berger, Elsa Morante, Victor Serge, Clarice Lispector. Surely these artists continued to imagine complexly, to—as it were—dream, even as they fought through their art against injustice?

If art of a certain strain is committed to process rather than product, it is especially difficult to sum up its final success. Was the art in the aftermath of Hiroshima successful? Was the art that characterized the takeover of Greenham Common successful? Were the *arpilleras* made by disenfranchised Chilean women successful?

Crisis art, dissident art, social activist art (largely synonymous) are perennial; one can't anticipate when an injustice or string of injustices, will invoke an art to register it.

But how will this art be appraised 40 years from now when the crisis that evoked it is no longer a factor?

Paradoxically, art produced rapidly under crisis conditions will sometimes have more lasting power and even esthetic appeal than the painstakingly created seemingly disinterested art that most people identify as quintessential. Crisis art has an energy and focus which more than compensate for its relative lack of refinement.

In the US there have been historical "moments"—the Quakers, the Abolitionists and Transcendentalists, the Thirties Marxists, the Sixties counter-culture, Act-Up in the late Eighties and early Nineties—but overall American writers have been contemptuous of socially-activist writing. It doesn't sell, it is more didactic than "esthetic." Moreover, why should artists be in a special position to address political crises?

Writers cultivate consciousness, contemplation, and in many instances learning. They view through a broader lens. If they have a reputation they can find a platform to make themselves heard and express their opinions precisely.

What good will it do? Wars, oppression, colonialism, profit-mania have been with us since human hegemony? And now authoritarian power is decentered, much less visible. Serious art of any kind has been rendered negligible in the market place, which in the US epitomizes the country's ethos.

With effort and intelligence, decentered power modules *can* be identified, as young dissidents and hackers have located and attempted to disable deliberately elusive nexuses of power and control.

Human history, however bloody and unjust, has not ceased; and, crucially, the planet we inhabit and have debauched is dying. Bangladesh is one of the world's poorest and most densely populated countries, with its people crammed into a delta of rivers that empties into the Bay of Bengal, which because of the Antarctic ice melt is behaving like an ocean, flooding ice paddies and entire villages. Animals and plants throughout the globe are becoming extinct rapidly. The sun, where the ozone layer is eroded, has become toxic. Lethal bacterial agents set loose from leveled rain forests or industrialized seas migrate into the general population.

Possibly the hardest factor for concerned younger artists to accept is that there will always be an incommensurateness between their imaginative efforts and results. The primary obligation is to not avert your eyes; to bear witness.

Freeze-Dry

Doctors are attempting to freeze-dry a severely disabled girl, 9-years-old, to keep her child-size at her parents' request. Born with static encephalopathy, she cannot walk or talk and has the mental capacity of a month-old infant.

Watch the child twist her mouth grotesquely and emit animal noises: [Video]

Anal Acrobats

Excrement is dead matter.

—Schopenhauer

Here I am, door bolted, doing what any hot-blooded, post-menopausal hetero male should be doing: trawling through XXX-rated sites on the Net.

These sites are gratis—I'm not dumb enough to pay $$ to view virtual porn.

We know the FBI, CIA, DEA, TSA, DHS…are monitoring paid subscribers to smut, even though most of the smut is owned (if you can trace the lineage) by sanitized corps like Disney, Walmart, Toys "R" Us, Starbucks, Google.

With HIV, like the global economy, in recession, many gay males are back to doing anal "bareback."

Why shouldn't they?

The curiosity here is how/why anal has become mainstream, even predominant, in the hetero community.

Check out this "Anal Acrobats" video I'm viewing right

now (I'm old but I multitask) with yellow golf balls functioning as outsized anal beads.

Three robotically gorgeous tattooed fems and a vaguely loutish male are manipulating three yellow golf balls from asshole to mouth to asshole to mouth...

Of course the anal fems have had their enemas before the action, get them a clean track.

But if there's some residual funk, no biggie, adds to the zest, right?

We are 12 years into the Millennium.

Beautiful people wannabes (who may be Tea-Partiers in real time) wax away their body hair.

Climate change, as it's euphemistically titled, has fucked the globe over faster than anyone could have anticipated.

Perpetrated by profit-mad industry.

Aided/abetted by cynical world leaders.

Which is more important: a polar bear cub dying in the Antarctic because of ice melt, or a hijacked vote?

Devastating tsunamis out of season or a good wax-job?

Shaved male heads are everywhere, a perverted monk universe.

Check that: reclusive monks have long practiced their own perversions.

Not Benedictines distilling an exotic liqueur with secret ingredients.

Not Franciscans raising cattle to be slaughtered.

The question I'm addressing obliquely is: Why is hetero

anal in such a groove at this time in this place even as I'm stroking my mouse?

Could it represent an unconscious, embodied acknowl-
edgement of *death* which is officially suppressed in the US?

Except in the instance of terrorists, homeless, and the in-
stitutionalized.

Those are vermin, obviously.

Murder them, piss on them, let them die.

Transform factories into prisons, privatized.

Surplus labor, cheapest you can find.

Mainstream Americans will live forever.

Or at least a thousand years, as the Austrian butcher with
the comical mustache claimed for the Reich.

Have you ever seen an American TV anchor with gray hair?

The anal acrobats I'm viewing online are obviously high on
coke, X, speed or some state of the art fusion.

They are hairless and prosthetic: faux boobs, of course, rhi-
noplasties, surgically inserted cheekbones, bad tattoos, photoshopped penises.

How deep is your ass-gape?

Not as deep as a grave, but t'will do.

Can we fit impoverished Bangladesh into your ass-gape,
150 million invisible souls, the country flooded with ice melt?

What about the Sudan?

In hetero porn the females do each other but not the
males—that is the code.

Occasionally two penises will carom one off the other as

when there is DP or the female is mouthing two cocks at once, but though males are secretly turned on by those erotic collisions they are not supposed to be.

Who established the hetero male code?

A literary fool might say Hemingway.

The Puritan church fathers established the hetero male code.

In the 17th century AD the Puritans discovered a country that was already occupied leveling God's wrath and voracious land-grabbing on the native inhabitants.

The Puritans' scions became our industrial and political chieftains in the name of Capital and their biblical God.

We have three impressive longhairs: a blonde, brunette and redhead; waxed hairless over the rest of their bodies.

The male's head is shaven, as I said, and his steroidal body is tattooed and hairless.

He is chiseled, he is hung, he is a stunt dick electronically generated.

In real time he is a couch potato with a receding hairline, minuscule penis, and affinity with numbers.

Currently he is unemployed.

His favorite porn fantasy is anal.

Especially in the US, Internet porn scoots rapidly from fetish to fetish, as though the viewer will turn back to his smart phone if the same species of porn is repeated for more than a week.

Peeing, squirting, teen, preggo, bestiality, gangbang, ebony, voyeur, gonzo, creampie, BDSM, BBW, hairy, butts, phat people, grannies, midgets, amputees, Asians, bisexual, trisexual, hentai.

blowjobs, handjobs, footjobs, deepthroat, vintage, retro, up-
skirt, lingerie, trans, webcams…have each had their time in the
electronic sun, but the perennial fave, the species with lasting
power, is still the "money shot."

Splat! Photoshopped cum shot from a big one right in yo' face…

Turning back to death, I feel certain that "snuff" porn would
outdo even the money shot, but viewing snuff, like viewing
child porn, is a "black op."

A felony if you're nabbed without connections.

Were snuff porn readily available on the Net its sublima-
tion into anal would not be a factor.

Who needs shit when we have death?

I am speculating.

Even more then deviant Weimar, when the natural world was
not palpably dying, our culture is pocked with noise, blandishments,
spectacle, shameless contradictions, brazen lies, squalid apologies.

We need extremity beyond extremity to dodge the collective torment we are forbidden to acknowledge.

Tsunamis and massive nuclear spills, as in Japan, will get
us grooving, but tragedy on that scale gets old fast.

Wars and "rendition" camps, called "black sites," are cool,
especially with both legislated and improvised torture, as in
Abu Ghraib and Gitmo.

NFL football with its crippling hits viewed and re-viewed
in hi-def slo-mo provides some small relief.

X-games and mixed martial arts are sleek when you're in
the mood.

Hyper-violent movies with CGI seem to work in part for kids with ADD and for stupid adults.

None of these is enough.

Death's smirk looms like a palimpsest behind the TV anchor's forced smile, cosmetic surgery, dyed yellow hair.

Addressing climate change even at the 11th hour is inadmissible.

Readmitting the noun "compassion" into the global lexicon is inadmissible.

Unless it is yet another acronym: *Cum-Passion*.

Collective suicide is officially beyond the pale, meaning that it is exclusively reserved for the colored poor ideally from "third world" countries.

Hence our current addiction to hetero anal acrobatics online, as graphically (obliquely) inscribed above.

Pet Girl

A British bus company apologized to a girl who is led around on a leash by her boyfriend after one of its drivers allegedly said, "We don't let freaks and dogs ride," and threw her off the bus.

Dressed in Goth-style clothes with a silver neckband attached to a long silver lead, the girl, 18, said she was the "pet" of her 25-year-old fiancé.

"I don't cook, I don't clean, I don't do anything or go anywhere without my master. To you it's strange but it's my culture and my choice. It isn't hurting anyone."

Animals

I am weary of being human.
—Clarice Lispector

At the base of a winding stair leading to Samadhi resides an amorphous creature known as A Bao A Qu, abnormally sensitive to the frailties of humankind.

The creature dozes uneasily until the pilgrim approaches, at which time a fire within the creature sparks and its amoebic body commences to assume form.

The pilgrim mounts the stair and the creature follows silently, becoming by degrees bluish and resembling an elephant.

It will achieve its ultimate form as Sri Ganesh only at the summit when the pilgrim has attained enlightenment.

Otherwise, the creature hesitates at the penultimate step and moans.

As the failed pilgrim descends the stair the creature tumbles to the first step, weary and shapeless.

A Bao A Qu awaits the approach of the next pilgrim.

It is said that no human has ever attained the summit.*

The elephants are enraged.

Trampling through hamlets in Africa, India, Nepal, Sri Lanka.

One elephant, murdered in Nepal, was found to have human remains in her stomach.

Elephants' brains are denser than humans'.

The temporal lobes associated with memory are more complexly developed than in humans.

Vastly more space for remembering.

In a functional world an elephant would kill herself before savaging a toxic human.

Poachers murder elephants for their tusks purported to grant virility.

Murder rhinos for the same reason.

Antelopes and wildebeests for the same reason.

There will be no more granting in Africa, India, Nepal, Sri Lanka.

Impotence, like industrial poison, is global.

Highly developed cerebral cortex humans cannot remember one ethnocide from another.

Sri Ganesh, elephant-son of Lord Shiva, is the remover of obstacles, emblem of good fortune.

When good fortune did not signify war mania, material gain beyond necessity.

When was that?

Elephants are deleted along with whales and dolphins.

If speech is a measure of intelligence, elephant-dolphin speech is beyond human comprehension.

Lispector writes:

When I see my horse running through the field I want to lean my head against his vigorous velvety neck and tell him the story of my life.

The wound dresser writes:

If I could I would live with the animals.

They do not wage war, exile or murder the innocent for money. They do not extort surplus labor for surplus value.

They do not exhibit overweening ambition, moronic bravura.

They do not use Skype or smart phones to have virtual sex then whine about their condition.

A rabbit shrieking in agony is no less than a billionaire banker.

Last week, 30 Tibetan Buddhists in Gloucester, Massachusetts purchased 534 lobsters from a seafood wholesaler, sprayed the lobsters with blessed water, clipped the bands binding their claws and released them one by one into the sea.

The Buddhists were observing Chokhor Duchen, Wheel Turning Day, the anniversary of Buddha's first sermon.

A polar bear and her cub trek 900 miles south from the Arctic ice melt to find food, dying en route.

A mountain lion from North Dakota somehow finds its way to wealthy Connecticut, where it is murdered.

Coyotes upend trashcans in Delaware and Rhode Island.

The nearly extinct kit fox makes the fatal mistake of straying too close to humans.

A great blue heron is stranded in the Mohave desert.

A single California quail is moored in Washington State near the Pacific.

Everyone has at least one dog, pure bred, in my upscale neighborhood.

(I'm a renter).

Nearby is a racetrack where injured million-dollar thoroughbreds are put down after each race.

A century after Upton Sinclair's "Jungle," cattle in coffin-like enclosures are shot with chemicals, tormented before and during slaughter.

Sharks, crocodiles and rattlers are goaded and murdered for spectacle, their murderers displaying the derring-do we're cued to applaud in elite "Seals" and black ops who war in third world countries for profit & entertainment.

When did we become a culture of ten-year-olds?

When surplus profit metastasized electronically.

What do we do next?

Pray, dream, huddle together, weep, kill back, follow our seeming dharma unquestioningly.

The warrior wars, priest prays, shopkeeper merchandizes.

As in the Bhagavad Gita.

Gandhi, devotee of Lord Rama, disobeyed the injunction.

Born into a shopkeeper caste, he fought peaceably for independence.

On behalf of India's "untouchables."

He was sometimes unkind to Kasturba, his wife.

Churchill called him "that naked little fakir."

Assassinated at last by a devout Brahmin who despised those who did not despise untouchables.

Gandhi's last word as he died was reportedly "Ram."

Lord Rama, whose animal familiar was Sri Hanuman, a monkey, infinitely superior to human kind.

Two nights ago I dreamt that an enormous crocodile was sheltering a naked infant in its wide-open reptilian jaws.

The infant was Caucasian.

Witnessing humans were incensed.

If they murdered the monster they would have to murder the child.

A congress was convened and three "wise" men were dispatched to the scene.

That is where the dream ended.

*After Borges

Fear

And you aren't afraid?
I was before. Not now.
What happened?
Cognac. It works on fear.
I drink two glasses every afternoon.
You do not drink?
I drink vodka.
There's no comparison.
After cognac you feel clear. Unafraid.
Only then will you permit yourself to be merciful.

Iso

The skies are raining blackbirds.

Thousands of red-winged blackbirds (*Angelaius phoeniceus*) fall from the sky round midnight in Mississippi state as we frenzy into year 2012.

Maya prophecies say this is the end-year; they do not mention Mississippi.

He's an old guy. Call him Qa. He's waiting it out alone.

He blows blues on his trombone.

Lies on the couch, dozes, dreams.

"Hellhound blues fallin' down like hail."

Robert Johnson, right?

Qa plays Robert Johnson, born and died on the Delta.

He lays the bone down and sings the words.

He sips chamomile tea.

Isolation is hard, old and iso are harder.

Unfriend your fair-weather friends asap.

Alone is to be alien.

One is alienated in any case.

Alienation stings but is good medicine.

Look at Robert Johnson.

Look at Oedipus after he puts out his eyes.

If he's old and alone does he do a lot of wanking?

Say what?

Qa. If he's old and alone does he do a lot of wanking?

He blows the trombone.

Delta blues, birds rain from the sky.

Lies on the couch, sips chamomile tea.

Dozes, dreams.

What kind of dreams?

Beasts enraged, ice breaking.

Didn't Qa say he means to live forever?

Not in this infected globe.

Online.

He's an ancient virus seeking left-handed software.

Do you know *The Left Handed Gun*?

Arthur Penn, 1958. Paul Newman plays lefty.

Paul Newman was the best Jewish cowboy in Hollywood.

Eli Wallach would be next, plug-ugly in those Sergio Leone opera buffa westerns contra pretty Clint Eastwood.

I heard Clint Eastwood was gay.

You know what "buffa" is, right?

Clown. Buffoon.

The global village is buffa.

Eurozone too.

IMF and CIA and DNS too.

Shoot me another acronym.

IPO.

Buffa.

Terrorists are out there.

Crocs, sharks, sex-addicts, rattlers, adolescent hackers, Muslim Jihadists, serial killers, earth-firsters, inner city rappers, Mexicans without green cards, dissident artists…

Dissident who?

Illegal aliens.

Qa's bros and sisters when he dreams.

Awake more or less he's iso, blows trombone.

Delta blues, after Robert Johnson.

Blackbirds rain from the sky.

He lies on the couch.

Sips chamomile tea.

Dozes, dreams.

He grunts and snores, kicks, moans, cries out.

Qa does all that?

He's an old guy, alone.

Asleep, he goes through the whole nine.

Awake, he puts words down on paper.

This and the other about the end of the end.

Don't ask him to describe it.

He writes, plays the bone, sings Robert Johnson?

That's way cool for an old guy.

Qa envies the psychopath.

Does his shit / don't give a shit.

No past, no future, just vibrating now.

No way does he look his age.

Qa, you mean?

Except for his hands.

You remember *La Femme Nikita?*

Luc Besson, 1990.

Jeanne Moreau, worldly femme, informs youthful Nikita that you may look young, but not the hands.

Hands give you away.

Qa will wear ivory satin gloves like Lon Chaney in *Phantom of the Opera*.

He won't cover his face.

He's a clean old dissident.

Tens of thousands of frogs born maimed.

They point to the futureless future.

To be old, iso, abandoned to the State, Fed, private sector, "assisted living" with or without your bone, points to the futureless future.

What would he—Qa—recommend?

A potent agent such as Oxycontin but not addictive and won't scramble consciousness, turn users into zombies.

True, one hears nice things about zombies.

Scrambling consciousness may be the best of the worst.

Writing about opium, Jean Cocteau appealed to scientists to modify the toxicity while maintaining the glow.

No chance.

On depleted earth glow is no-go.

Even as we spin out of orbit.

Too many creatures dreaming, moving sideways, promote chaos.

There is, naturally, a difference between extemporaneous and systemic chaos.

Licit and illicit terror.

Armed drones in Disneyworld, for example.

That's good, right?

The "1 percent": Watch them walk without swinging their arms.

They're speaking in Esperanto on their mobiles.

Ceaseless buzz of "information."

Qa blows Robert Johnson blues on his trombone.

Puts the bone down, sings a little.

Lies on his couch.

Dozes, dreams.

End of the end.

He'll wait it out.

Qa, I mean.

Come view the red-winged blackbirds rain from the skies.

Sacrifice
(Directed by Andrei Tarkovsky, 1986)

Barren windswept island off the south coast of Sweden.

Ingmar Bergman landscape.

Bergman's old colleague, Erland Josephson, plays Alexander, pensioner, former writer with an unfaithful wife and young child, who is compelled to sacrifice.

His wife and child?

Himself.

His sole option.

The diseased earth is in the throes of dying.

Retreat or immersion.

No half-measures.

Retreat is illusory, immersion is sacrifice.

Does his sacrifice bear fruit?

He lies with the good "witch," devotee of Mother Mary.
He sets fire to his house.
He is forcibly restrained.
Transported to the institution where suffering is imposed.
Legislated torment.
But the war that would holocaust the diseased earth is nulli-
fied.
Time backs up.
Literally.
Temporary reprieve.

Why "temporary?"

Open your eyes.

Does it matter that Alexander is a failed writer?

Not failed. Ceased to write.
The joy—where there is joy—is in the art-making.
If that dies nothing remains but retreat or sacrifice.

Sacrifice imitates Christ whether or not it is fruitful?
Didn't Artaud, Sade, even Hitler, sacrifice in their own ways?

Not Hitler.

The other two—arguably.

Is the diseased earth irreparable?

You ask me or Tarkovsky?

Tarkovsky.

Man and his institutions will not cease to filthy o'er the earth.
Profiting all the while.
The diseased earth can be cleansed solely by God's grace.

Sacrifice?

Though not animals, not trees.
Not humans, unless the sacrifice is willed, chosen.

Did the "chosen people" will their "sacrifice"?
Their holocaust?

The Jews?

The Jews.

I think of Mahler, Jew despite his baptism.
Mahler had the birds killed outside his dacha to claim the silence he needed to compose *Song of the Earth.*

That was the rumor.

Why bring up Mahler?

He comes to me.

What happens if one's sacrifice amounts to nothing?

Nothing happens.

It is the gesture that vibrates irrespective of results.
Even if the gesture costs your life.
But what if it costs the lives of others?
I think of John Brown's raid on Harpers Ferry—two of his sons killed.
Brown hanged for treason.

Weird John Brown.
"Weird" is Melville's word, meaning *fated*.
In Melville's poem the hanging shroud covers John Brown's face but not his "streaming beard" which juts sideways foretelling the meteoric energy of the anti-slave movement to come.

Slavery has not been abolished. It is everywhere in numberless guises.

Yes.

It is not the climax, then, but the process.
Yours is a bleak view of the world.

Made world.
The world itself—what remains of it—is a blessing reviled.

Old Testament.
You sound like weird John Brown.

Without sacrifice.

Why without?

I could have made my opportunity but hesitated.

Back in the day you considered joining the Weather Underground.
Becoming a "human shield" in the Palestinian territories.
Joining the flotilla delivering supplies to blockaded Gaza.

I grieved from a safe distance.

You know about Pasolini's homosexual relations with rough
young boys in the Rome ghettos.
Maybe you heard the odd story?
That he deliberately provoked the boys to beat and murder him
so that the debased photo with his face battered, trousers at his
knees, sex exposed, would testify to our collective squalor.

Presumably he envisioned it as a sacrificial or—better—sha-
manic act.

Weird story, but in Pasolini's instance, not implausible.

I admire Pasolini however he choreographed his death.

How does one distinguish narcissism from sacrifice?

They can be indistinguishable.

You are a writer sans frontiere.
Doesn't your writing count?

Count?

As a species of sacrifice?

I don't know.

Bride of Frankenstein
(Directed by James Whale, 1935)

Shelley: death by water.

Byron: death in battle (sort of).

Mary Shelley, the poet's wife, Wollstonecraft's daughter, outlives her royal paramours, continues to write, but nothing with the purchase of *Frankenstein: The Modern Prometheus*.

Nor will Mary Shelley's monster die for as long as godless demi-creators aspire to Godhood.

In a prologue we view the three in a Geneva castle discussing Mary's monster.

Byron, with the most famous clubfoot in literature, limps but wears mauve pantaloons and adores hearing his own voice.

Shelley, possibly thinking of Plato, is in an amiable fog.

No worries: Mary Shelley will hold her own with those immortal bounders.

And now James Whale's super flick unfurls.

What of Dr. Pretorius?

Played by James Whale's fave: the inimitable high-camp Ernest Thesiger.

Pretorius adores gin.

In his scholar's skullcap, together with Henry Frankenstein, he proposes a toast to "Gods and Monsters."

Frankenstein hired louts to raid graves for fresh corpses.

Pretorius claims to have grown his souls from "cultures."

When I hear the word culture, I reach for my iphone.

Ensemble, aided by a providential storm, Frankenstein-Pretorius create a prospective monster's bride.

Elsa Lanchester does double-duty, as Mary Shelley and with art-deco electrified hair, the monster's bride.

Truly, she is better off with monster Karloff than with her husband, real-time Charles Laughton, formidably ugly.

Yearly, he would read Dickens' *A Christmas Carol* on the Ed Sullivan variety show.

He was known to play with himself on the set and didn't like girls.

The monster is keen on girls, platonically of course.

Alas, the bride loathes the monster.

She prefers the Baron, Henry Frankenstein.

She is upwardly mobile.

Just like a womanoid.

Predictably, the villagers with their obligatory torches, moni-
tored by the doltish burgomaster, crucify the monster—or
just about.
Only the blind hermit, who plays Ave Maria on the violin, cot-
tons to the creature, takes him in.
Bandages the hurt-by-humans monster.
Teaches him to grunt-speak.
Refined music and charity.
Byron possessed one but not the other.
It was rumored that once, Byron, drunk and in high dud-
geon, displayed his penis in the House of Lords, then
proceeded to urinate from a balcony onto the head of the
Viscount something-or-other who had previously expressed
an unflattering word about Byron's verses.
He was given to fat, hence swam the Hellespont, employing
breaststroke solely.

That was long before the crawl, right?

He also fornicated, vomited, took laxatives.
Man-child Shelley, stooped, goofyish, proves unexpectedly virile.
Incomprehensible angel.
In the flick's climax the ardent monster and revolted bride per-
ish together, along with Dr. Pretorius.
Meanwhile, the hubristic Baron slinks away to be reincarnated

into the emperor of profiles, Basil Rathbone, in the next segment, when Karloff, the monster himself, is reborn.

Monsters perish, ultimately.
Monstrous acts fester.

Things to Do

Ingest MDMA (Ecstasy in American English).

Uncut.

Have a warm bath while it comes on, working its way up through the top of your skull.

Sit naked, cross-legged on the Navajo rug loving the world and everything in it.

For how long?

Two hours and 45 minutes.

Truth-Force

Polling los pobres

"I've read the report."

"You know the situation. It has nothing to with sentiment; the torturer never showed any. It has nothing to do with what the junta refers to as law and order. It has to do with justice. Yes or no?"

"Yes."

"I've read the report."

"You know the situation. It has nothing to with sentiment; the torturer never showed any. It has nothing to do with what the junta refers to as law and order. It has to do with justice. Yes or no?"

"Yes."

"I've read the report."

"You know the situation. It has nothing to with sentiment;

the torturer never showed any. It has nothing to do with what the junta refers to as law and order. It has to do with justice. Yes or no?"

"*Yes.*"

"*I've read the report.*"

"You know the situation. It has nothing to with sentiment; the torturer never showed any. It has nothing to do with what the junta refers to as law and order. It has to do with justice. Yes or no?"

"*Yes.*"

The preceding exchanges are in Spanish and take place on a local tram. One by one, the *compañero* boards the tram, sits by the questioner, repeats the coded sentence, *I've read the report*, then casts his or her vote. The *compañero* leaves and is replaced by another. The same exchange occurs on trams throughout the city. The question is whether to execute the torturer or release him.

Yes signifies execution.

Eight insurgents (as they're called in the junta-controlled media), question a total of 310 men and women of various ages, most of them poor, each connected one way or another with the "insurgency."

Each of the eight questioners records the responses on an interior page of *Libertad*, the junta's flagship newspaper.

The 310 responses are unanimously in the affirmative.

Uprooting Trees

The governing junta seized power unlawfully, and the official torturer who is kidnapped and soon to be executed was imported from a colonialist "first-world" country thousands of miles to the north.

The imported torturer was loosely disguised as an aid agency official to undeveloped or underdeveloped or primitive or third-world (there are many comparable designations) countries.

The imported torturer's charge: instruct the junta police and Republican Guard in the newest most technologically advanced methods of interrogation and torture including how to "disappear" rebellious citizens, the majority poor, many indigenous.

(The indigenous constitute the earliest citizens whose ancestors inhabited the country when it was "discovered" by Europeans in armor—the junta's alleged ancestors).

The torturer in his own developed country was chief of police in a large southwestern city close to the Mexican border. Employing methods old and new, his police force menaced, murdered and disappeared Mexican immigrants, whom they call "illegal aliens." Hence the executioner's imperfect knowledge of Spanish.

Imperfect is good enough.

Before polling its members on the execution, the insurgents called on the junta to exchange its 189 political prisoners for the kidnapped torturer.

The request was denied.

Would the all-powerful colonialist country from which the torturer came intervene?

No, the all-powerful colonialist country would use his execution (he possessed a devoted wife and five children) as further propaganda against the insurgency, then send another professional torturer (with a devoted wife and four or five children) to replace him, even as the professional torturer who preceded the current torturer (with a devoted wife and four children) had been kidnapped and executed by insurgents.

Did professional torturers with devoted wives and four or five children grow on trees up there in that all-powerful country?

No, because the trees were uprooted to erect prisons, sports stadiums and condominiums.

Dream

He was not the imported torturer but a junta police officer, one of the imported torturer's trainees.

He said to me: "Since you refuse to talk we will make you dream."

I understood what he meant, but not the extent of it.

Do you know how it feels to have electric shock applied to your genitals?

They strip you and wrap wet rags up and down your body.

They push you into the pit filled with shit and piss and blood and vomit where they tortured and murdered your *compañeros*.

You'd expect the electric shock to feel like catching hold of a live wire with your fingers.

One might tolerate that.

This is a hundred times worse.

The pain is heightened in the parts of the body that hold liquids.

Shocking the genitals feels like they're pulling your kidneys and bladder out with red-hot tongs.

They move the electrodes up and down the body.

When the electrodes are applied to the heart you cannot speak or breathe.

They keep the wet rags on you all the time to increase the pain.

When the rags dry they wet them again.

All the time the interrogation continues.

I didn't know until inmate *compañeros* told me afterwards that they wept to hear me tortured.

I screamed and wailed, they told me.

It was a pain like nothing else.

Pain beyond pain.

Truth-Force

"Am I right to say that the revolutionary response was milder at first than it became? That your response was initially modeled on Gandhi's non-violent Satyagraha, sometimes translated as truth-force?"

"That's accurate, yes."

"Did your response become more violent by degree or was the turn to violence sudden?"

"By degree. We discussed and argued about it at meetings. But the tortures and disappeared, the mass executions in the football stadiums, the everyday cruelties toward the people—even the Gandhian *compañeros* came to recognize that if we wanted to exert any political force we would need to spill their blood as they spilled the blood of the innocent."

"Did any of the *compañeros* drop out at that juncture?"

"No. But it was a moment of truth for all of us. It was very hard to learn to think like assassins. Even righteous assassins. Gandhi was fighting the British in India. If the Indian colonialists had been Afrikaans, say, or Germans, his nonviolence would not have worked."

"You don't think so?"

"When, during the Nazi holocaust, Gandhi was asked what he would say to the Jews who were being led to the gas, he said he would counsel them to look their assailants in the eye. Gandhi was a great leader, but here he was wrong. You look a Nazi in the eye and he will pluck it out. And if you were to fast in protest, as Gandhi so often did with success, the Afrikaans or Nazis would fast you to death."

"So you became assassins yourself. Righteous assassins."

"Yes. The context demanded it. Unless we wanted to give up the struggle, there was no other way.

"Approximately how many revolutionary *compañeros* are there?"

"In our country we are nearly a thousand active fighters, men and women, with many thousands of people at large supporting us. In neighboring countries, we have similar numbers."

"Do you expect to finally win?"

"Absolutely. But even when we win the work must continue. Che—and Trotsky before him—called for unceasing revolution."

"That would be very hard to sustain."

"True."

"And yourself: does an early violent death frighten you?"

"Living under this filthy, greedy, murdering junta is death, day after day. My own death will come when it comes."

Eyes

Avert your eyes.

Don't avert your eyes.

Avert your eyes.

Don't avert your eyes.

Avert your eyes.

Don't avert your eyes.

Avert your eyes.

Don't avert your eyes.

Avert your eyes.

Don't avert your eyes.

Avert your eyes.

Don't avert your eyes.

Avert your eyes.

Don't avert your eyes.

Avert your eyes.

Don't avert your eyes.

Avert your eyes.

Don't avert your eyes.

Avert your eyes.

Don't avert your eyes.

Avert your eyes.

Don't avert your eyes.

Hijab

French technocrat and Muslim teenager
at the entrance to the lycée outside Paris

> *Bonjour, Mlle.*
>
> *You are required to remove your headscarf.*
>
> Bonjour, Monsieur.
>
> I never remove the hijab in public.
>
> *This is a state-supported lycée, Mlle.*
>
> *It is not a mosque.*
>
> *It is not a souk.*
>
> *In France we maintain separation of church and state.*
>
> *That is established policy*
>
> We understood the established policy to be cohabitation.

Former colonies cohabiting with their benefactors—you
white French—with their native customs intact.

Cohabitation you virtuously opposed to assimilation, such
as the United States promotes, where everyone is expected to

staple the American flag to their forehead, indistinguishable one from the other.

Mlle, the correct opposition is not between cohabitation and assimilation but between a secular state such as we have in France and a theocracy.

Is the US then a theocracy?

Without question.

Two global reprobates slouching
outside the Bourse, in Paris

Who set the Reichstag fire in 1933 and as a consequence facilitated Hitler?

The Jew.

Who toppled the World Trade Center in 2001 and as a consequence facilitated Bush?

The Muslim.

Who "emigrated mentally" while living unmolested in Nazi Germany and Austria?

Aryan intellectuals and artists.

Who, post 9/11, duct-taped American intellectuals and artists into the condominiums of their minds?

The crusading US government.

Taking a page from their Red-baiting McCarthy era.

The US later apologized for McCarthyism as an unfortunate departure from capitalist democracy's firmest values.

The US apologized for interning Japanese-Americans, but then did it again with Muslim-Americans.

9/11 gave them the excuse to reinvent history.

As farce.

Is genocide farce?

French technocrat and Muslim teenager

at the entrance to the lycée outside Paris

Mlle, the ordinance is in place.

Nor does it refer exclusively to Muslims.

Conspicuous religious items of several kinds are prohibited.

Jews are forbidden to wear skullcaps.

Hindus are forbidden to paint their faces.

Christians are forbidden to wear visible crosses larger than three centimeters.

Are Catholic nuns forbidden to wear head coverings?

Catholic nuns would have gone beyond the lycée, Mlle.

The ordinance does not apply to education beyond the lycée.

Why not?

That should be self-evident, Mlle.

The intention of the ordinance is to instill the ideal of secular education in the young.

Before religious habits or customs become irreversible.

We have an obligation to care for children who enter the French public school system, and the fact is that young Muslim females are often coerced into wearing the headscarf.

Wearing the hijab is a fundamental principle of Sharia, Monsieur.

To assert that the hijab is forced on Muslim women is ignorant and paternalistic.

The "secularism" you are attempting to impose is yet another
sign of intolerance towards the growing Muslim community.

I refuse to engage in an argument about semantics, Mlle.

That is the way the ordinance reads.

Two global reprobates slouching
outside the Bourse, in Paris

When I say hijab what comes to mind?

The veil.

Taking the veil.

Entering the convent.

France, for example, is proud of its various orders of nuns,
"*les bonnes soeurs.*"

The sisters are picturesque; they don't disrupt the body
politic; they have an esthetic dimension.

In France that would be crucial.

I think too of raising the veil, uncovering.

Which invokes the practice of clitorectomy or infibulation.

What percentage of Islamic females worldwide are subjected to this practice?

No clue.

I wouldn't trust whatever estimates the "First World" puts out.

*What percentage of males worldwide are subjected to circum-
cision?*

Are clitorectomy and circumcision comparable?

You tell me.

Couldn't the veil also be identified with movement induced by natural forces?

The aeolian harp stroked by the wind.

Or unnatural forces: Separation from the madding crowd in homage to the creative imagination.

What does hijab signify to you?

The sacred prepuce of its white male leaders.

French technocrat and Muslim teenager
at the entrance to the lycée outside Paris

France—before Sarkozy—officially objected to the invasion of Iraq.

France officially objects to Israel's violent annexation of Palestine.

What France is doing in France to its female Muslim minority is no less poisonous.

One thing has nothing to do with another, Mlle.

The ordinance is unambiguous.

Islamic females of lycée age are required to remove their head and face coverings while in the lycée or on the grounds of the lycée.

Once you leave the lycée you may dress and do as you please.

So long as it is within the law.

Senegalese and Ivory Coast former subjects of lycée age are not required to remove their dashikis and bubas.

Tunisian, Algerian and Moroccan former subjects of lycée age are not required to remove their kaftans and jubbahs.

Caribbean former subjects of lycée age are not required to undo their dreadlocks.

It is just your orthodox Muslim females of lycée age who are required to remove their hijabs.

What is it about young Muslim females that intimidates their former colonial occupier?

You are imagining things, Mlle.

The official ordinance reads as indicated.

I do not propose to argue with you over niceties.

Two global reprobates slouching outside the Bourse, in Paris

Except for its Muslims and Jews, France is officially uncircumcised.

What if someone, not Muslim or Jew, elects to be circumcised?

Unless for reasons of health, which must be officially verified, he will have to do it outside the law.

On the subject of the prepuce, the hijab can also signify the formal body coverings of its political leaders, graduates of the same elite ecoles.

Have you noticed how indistinguishable France's presidents and prime ministers—Giscard, Pompidou, Mitterand, Chirac— look in their somber double-breasted suits?

Pale, stiff, punctilious, marmoreal.

Sarkozy isn't marmoreal.

Sarkozy is arboreal.

Was it William James who remarked that the sheerest of

veils separates the mundane, agitated, warring world from the world inhabited by the higher spirits?

Yet this sheer, transparent veil is so infrequently parted.

William James was American.

I don't read Americans.

William James's younger brother Henry was in his heart of hearts *un Francais de plaisir.*

The father, Henry senior, was a Swedenborgian.

Alice James, like Proust, was bedridden.

She wrote and dictated on her back.

Why don't you read Americans?

They are without history.

Virtually no lived history from which to draw.

Is that less privileged than having a long history but drawing the same opportunistic conclusions?

French technocrat and Muslim teenager
at the entrance to the lycée north of Paris

Mlle, I refuse to stand here arguing with you.

The ordinance is clear.

If you or any among you wish to dispute it, that should be done formally and lawfully.

You've repeated lawful several times.

Isn't it a fact that you formulate then implement laws as you choose, according to your own advantage?

All the time professing that these laws are immutable, engraved in stone by your Christian god?

Mlle, I have done my best to be courteous, even as you have insisted on arguing.

Now you have come dangerously close to blasphemy.

I hereby terminate this discussion.

Good day, Mlle.

You white upper class French fuss about courtesy, which you use to mask your hypocrisy.

Have you considered the repercussions your anti-Islamic ordinance will produce?

Good day, Monsieur.

Two global reprobates slouching outside the Bourse, in Paris

We were discussing the images invoked by the hijab, or veil.

We've cited nuns; prepuces; the somber formal wear of our leaders; music stirred by the wind; clitorectomy and circumcision; alienation in homage to the creative imagination; the sheer veil that according to William James separates elevated vision from the every day.

What about the now-defunct Red Chinese and their Bamboo Curtain?

The now-defunct Soviets and their Iron Curtain?

The privileged quartiers of Paris?

The gated communities of the USA, and increasingly the rest of the world, with its tiny minority of nervous rich.

Metastasized technology, where users are guided absolutely by their screen?

And now, world-wide—globally, as they say—we have our exponentially multiplying oppressed Muslim underclass.

Enraged and desperate behind their Muslim curtain.

Which could end up being the most horrific "veil" of all.

Agreed?

No.

I believe the greatest horrors will be wreaked by the other side.

*

A French woman who alleged she had been the subject of an anti-Semitic attack invented the story, police sources now say.

The admission came shortly after the she was taken into custody—four days after the alleged assault on a commuter train north of Paris.

The 24-year-old woman claimed six men accused her of being Jewish, then forcibly cut off her clothes with long knives and spray-painted swastikas on her nude body.

The woman, who is not Jewish, has been detained for falsely reporting a crime, state prosecutor Didier Merleau-Ponty told AFP news agency.

She could face up to six months in prison and an 8,000-euro ($11,000) fine if convicted.

The case has sparked widespread condemnation amid concerns that racist and anti-Semitic attacks are on the rise in France, which of course has a long and sordid history of such uprisings.

The men, described as North African and of indeterminate age, are also said to have deliberately upended the woman's 8-month-old infant from its stroller.

The infant fell on its head but was reportedly uninjured.

The woman claimed that some 20 people witnessed the attack but that nobody offered her support.

However, investigators, studying footage from surveillance cameras at the train station where the six alleged North African attackers were supposed to have exited, found no evidence to support the woman's claim.

Nor has a single witness come forth even after urgent appeals in the media.

Now police sources who requested anonymity say that under "firm questioning" the woman recanted her accusations.

She admitted cutting off her own clothes and spray-painting the swastikas on her naked body with the help of her boyfriend who is also in custody.

Presumably she spray-painted the front of her body and her boyfriend spray-painted the back.

Like her, the boyfriend is neither Jewish nor North African, but French and white.

Le Monde, the left-leaning French daily, reports that the young woman filed several complaints in the past about being the victim of racist violence.

The reputed brutality of the attack, its anti-Semitic character, and the fact that no one came to the woman's aid provoked outrage, adding to the growing concern over racist and anti-Semitic attacks.

President Nicolas Sarkozy, who condemned the alleged assault as "pitiless and reprehensible," vowed to deny clemency to any prisoner serving a sentence for a racist or anti-Semitic crime.

Government spokesman Jean-Chrétien Irigaray told RTL radio that the rising trend of anti-Semitic attacks was "a genuine evil" in France, even if the woman's case "proved to be imagined rather than real, as such."

Russian Roo

See the wizened humanoid in his motorized wheelchair flying a tattered American flag, the flag that maimed him in the war and afterwards.

Where?

My intention was: Delete the corrupt institutions that did him.
Disappear the robotic leaders.
Then disappear.
There were too many.
It was viral.

Disappear leaders how?

The revolting revolt.

Who?

The abused, the made-revolting.
The wizened humanoid in the motorized wheelchair flying his
tattered American flag.
Can you see him?

Where?

He fought for the flag only to be victimized by it.

You envision him and his kind revolting?
Pipe dream.

You're certain?

Nothing is certain.
You want to delete the corrupt leaders then disappear.
Disappear how?
Would you bleed?

Do you want to see me bleed?

Maybe.
Can I think about it?

React. Don't think.

Sorry.

Look now.
The wizened humanoid in the motorized wheelchair flying his tattered American flag.

Where?

In one of his autobiographical fragments, Graham Greene claims to have played Russian Roulette.
This was before he smoked opium in Vietnam and wrote *The Quiet American.*
He describes the opium process graphically.
More graphically than Cocteau, more than De Quincey.

What if Greene had lost at Russian Roulette?

He wouldn't have smoked opium in Vietnam and provided an admirable description.
He wouldn't have written about the cruel banality of colonialist wars in *The Quiet American.*

Is The Quiet American a great novel?

Don't be a fool.

Did Greene become addicted?

To war?
Technology?

To opium.

Not at all.
It reinforced his alienation.
Permitted him to see.
Licensed him to write.

*Was it to reinforce his alienation that he traveled to remote parts
of the world?*

Among other things.

And now?

World is globe.
Wilderness is real estate.
Wars and entertainment have gone viral.

That's the second time you've used "viral."
You're saying the artist needs separation to imagine.
*The buzz of spectacle post-millennium is ceaseless, without
boundary.*
There is no longer an outside.
But isn't crucial art still being created?

Crucial to whom?

Hedge fund managers.
I can't tell you exactly.
To whom was Graham Greene's art crucial in the 40s and 50s?

To a public that could read and occasionally think.
Occasionally feel.

George Orwell detested Greene.
He said Greene could have written the same "exotic" novels had
he remained in London.

Presented as a reformer, Orwell was a puritan.
Prodigious hater of deviation.

Except for you and writers like you he is scarcely remembered.
Graham Greene.

Which signifies?

He is no longer crucial.
Possibly he was never as crucial as you make him out.
You admire him because of the Russian roulette and opium.
Because of his venturesome traveling and sexing.
Is it your contention that every artist should play Russian

Roulette, then if he or she survives travel to the ends of the globe
and smoke opium?

Without question.

Traveling these days—by air especially—is bestial.

There are ways.

By motorized wheelchair, I know.
What happens if the Russian Roo is "successful"?

I thought I responded to that.
Then s/he does not get to travel bestially, smoke opium, have
sex, make art.

Pity.

Can you see him now?
The wizened humanoid in the motorized wheelchair flying his
tattered American flag?

Where?

Things to Do

Find work as a baggage handler for a major airliner. Secretly rummage through lost or delayed luggage. Collect female hair from brushes, combs, intimate wear. Bag the hair in transparent plastic, label it. Encode your fantasies of the hair-owner's most intimate gestures on your smart phone.

Salvation Mountain

Jesus came to him in the cab of a Datsun long bed pickup.

Gloomy Monday, ten minutes before midnight, March 3, 1973, St. Johnsbury, Vermont.

Dewey Birdsong was parked in his truck because he'd run out of money and had no place to go.

He usually made enough to get by shoveling snow in the long winters.

But this winter was uncommonly dry so he couldn't afford to rent a room by the week as was his custom.

It was cold in the truck and he couldn't sleep.

To keep his mind off the cold he prayed to Jesus, which he'd done before on occasion.

This time he prayed aloud, insistently.

Finally he dozed and he dreamed.

It was not a dream but a vision.

Lord Jesus came to him and said:

Go to the end of the earth and construct a mountain to testify to me.

It will be called Salvation Mountain.

But first you must learn to fly like a bird.

Three days later Dewey, with borrowed money, was driving west.

He stopped in Newton, Iowa, where he got work as a farm-hand along with room and board.

In his spare time he set about building a hot air balloon so that he could learn to fly like a bird.

He spent seven years building the balloon from nylon scraps and Styrofoam plastic harvested from dumpsters.

Painted bright orange, the balloon bore the billboard-sized message that God is Love, which Dewey inscribed in black latex house paint.

The problem was the balloon was about nine stories high and Dewey could not get it off the ground.

So he bid farewell to the Iowa farmer, his employer and landlord for the last seven years.

He mounted the balloon on an old Ford flatbed truck and drove west to the most desolate place he could find that was more or less inhabitable.

The southeast tip of California.

An outpost called Slab City, in the Mojave Desert, between Niland and the Chocolate Mountains, a few miles east of the massive inland Salton Sea.

There he tried again to loft the balloon and this time was successful.

He steered it to the Salton Sea, then farther west to the Pacific.

Then he turned the balloon around and headed back east where it suddenly lost altitude and plummeted to the hard desert floor.

Amazingly, Dewey survived unhurt.

He said, "I just rutted out here, so I figured I'd stay put."

Having at last flown, Dewey Birdsong ceased working on the balloon and turned his full attention to constructing a mountain in the slabs of the Mojave Desert.

Located on the former Camp Locust Marine Corps base due east of Niland, Slab City received its name from the cement slab remains of the former base buildings.

The slabs made convenient parking blocks for RVs, SUVs pickup trucks, and abandoned school busses.

Between November and April more than 3000 "snowbirds," pensioners, and assorted misfits are drawn to the ungoverned life in the Slab City desert.

They don't pay taxes or fees of any kind.

Who would pay for squatting at the end of the earth, where summer comes in March, lasts through October and the temperature climbs to 115 degrees?

Where there is no electricity, running water, sanitation, or medical facilities.

Where the stench from the decomposing sea is close to overwhelming for miles around.

During World War 2, General Patton used the desert base for war games to simulate the African campaign he would wage against Rommel.

Later the Enola Gray crew would practice for Hiroshima by releasing dummy A bombs into the Salton Sea.

Though the Marine Corps base that occupied Slab City is abandoned, the US army still drops bombs at a desert "test site" three or four miles away.

Bombay Beach, the bereft hamlet north of Niland, takes its name not from its Bombay, India-like setting on the fetid sea but from the bombs that explode intermittently to the east.

Dewey Birdsong was fond of saying that he had difficulty drawing a straight line.

But after Jesus came to him in the Datsun long bed pickup on that freezing Vermont night he became infused not only with God but with an architecture that testified to God.

Dewey said that even now, 30-something years after beginning the construction of Salvation Mountain, he never knew what he was going to paint or sculpt until he held the paintbrush or chisel in his hand and Jesus instructed him.

Occasionally he would have to appeal out loud to Jesus to guide his hand.

After working on the mountain for three years it collapsed in a windstorm.

Dewey cleared away the debris and began again, substituting clay for sand and making other construction alterations.

Dewey said, "With Jesus in me I can make a hundred mistakes and start all over with exactly the same enthusiasm."

Dewey constructed the mountain out of straw bales covered in adobe, that is, a mixture of clay soil, chopped straw, and water.

He painted phrases from Scripture, biblical injunctions, birds, flowers and allegorical figures; layer on layer in a delirious medley of colors.

Dewey estimates that he's used about forty thousand gallons of paint, all donated.

Eighty-years-old now, he still wakes up at five am, drinks a glass of water and gets to work.

He climbs the ladder and hoists bales of hay into large clefts in the mountain which he cements with adobe.

In one large cleft he actually managed to insert the ruins of a mature ironwood tree, roots and all.

It functions as a buttress for the adobe overlay.

Still on the ladder, Dewey paints and sculpts his biblical quotations, flowers, and symbolic figures on to the adobe.

He works until 11 or 11:30.

The rest of the day is given over to reading scripture, feeding his animals (cats and dogs that people abandoned), greeting and giving tours to visitors.

If it cools off a little at dusk he will work on the mountain for another hour or so.

A twenty foot stone cross painted bright pink marks the highest point of Salvation Mountain.

The centerpiece, just beneath the cross, is a massive red heart with the multicolored message: **JESUS, I'M A SINNER, PLEASE COME UPON MY BODY AND INTO MY HEART**.

Dewey carved steps into the mountain's side for pilgrims to scale and examine the display from different angles.

He constructed kivas or grottos at the base of the mountain, where pilgrims can rest away from the sun.

He himself lives in an old Dodge pickup with a shell, which was donated.

He still owns the Ford Flatbed truck which he drove west from Newton, Iowa.

Someone donated an ancient school bus and a bicycle.

Another Samaritan donated a moped.

Dewey has painted and inscribed all of these vehicles with colorful biblical quotations and commands.

Dewey Birdsong, in his wide-brimmed straw hat, is tall, rail-thin, slightly stooped, with an eagle-nose, deeply sunburned face and illuminated blue eyes under shaggy white brows.

When he talks with you in his soft voice he tends to look over your head, beyond you.

Despite the onerous work and his advanced age his long hands are slim and mostly unlined.

***

Dewey, you dreamt of Jesus in your Datsun pickup on the other side of the continent nearly forty years ago.

That, you've said, marked the beginning of your quest.

Do you still dream of Jesus when you sleep at night?

Jesus is with me all day while I work.
At night I'm so bone-tired I sleep real deep.
But I also float.

In what sense?

The way it is when I climb the ladder with the bale and the
adobe.
Only there's no ladder.
And I don't feel any of the weight of the bale and the clay.

Jesus is levitating you, making you float?

Yes sir.

*Jesus tells you what to paint on the mountain the following
morning?*

No, huh-uh.
That comes when I'm on the ladder working.

How does Jesus communicate to you?
Through words?

Not exactly.

The Slabs draw a lot of different people.
Snowbirds, the homeless, even some dangerous types.
Outlaws, bikers, militia.
How have the people in and around the Slabs responded to
Salvation Mountain?

Oh, real good.

Lots of Christian folks have expressed themselves very positive about the mountain.

Even the non-believers, they've been supportive to the mountain.

Folks buy me coffee and donuts in the restaurants.

People buy me groceries.

I don't ask.

I can turn my back and there'll be groceries and two cans of paint right next to my truck.

See, it ain't me.

It's God's mountain working through me.

I didn't see a church in Niland or Bombay Beach.
Where are the nearest evangelical churches?

Well, there's one up in Mecca, just north of Salton City.

Another down there in Brawley.

But I've never went.

My church is right here.

Your mountain.

Jesus' mountain.

I'm just real fortunate he chose me to build it.

Because without him I could not even draw a straight line.

Why do you think Jesus chose you rather than, say, an artist or sculptor with knowledge and experience?

I've asked myself that same question.

I always kinda figured that God scraped the bottom of the barrel to have me build his mountain.

Maybe he just wanted to prove he could pick somebody that really couldn't do it and then have him do it. **[laughs]**

Man, I was here without state permission.

The county didn't never give me permission.

I had no right to be here at all.

But God got it done for me.

I think maybe to testify to his faith in poor folks.

The poor and the ignorant, like me.

Was it ten or a dozen years ago that county supervisors called Salvation Mountain a "toxic nightmare" because of the leaded paint you used?

They talked about bulldozing the mountain and burying it in a hazardous-waste site on an Indian reservation in Nevada.

Has that problem with the supervisors been resolved?

Oh, sure.

Senator Barbara Boxer wrote to the supervisors on behalf of the mountain.

So did twenty-five museum directors from acrost the country.

You see, I never knew much about politicians.

They thought they could push me over easy because I'm clumsy, awkward, I've got no money.

But once they realized they were wrong, they backed off.

I still believe American politicians are better than in most countries.

I know you paint and sculpt every day.
Do you eat every day or do you sometimes fast?

I eat, but not much.

I used to fast but now I don't have the strength to fast after climbing the ladder and working in the sun.

It gets pretty darn hot out here.

What do you eat?

Pretty much what good folks donate.

Whatever groceries I find by my truck, that's what I eat.

I never fussed about food, even when I was young.

I never had enough money to fuss.

I never went to school the way everyone does these days.

I was ignorant, like I said.

I'm still ignorant.

But I love Jesus and through his grace I am building this mountain.

But it is actually Jesus building it with my hands.

You've become famous, Dewey.

Salvation Mountain is reproduced in art books both in this country and Europe.

You receive hundreds of visitors.

They give you donations.

What do you do with the donated money?

Well, I used to keep it in my truck.

But then I was robbed a few times.

[smiles and shrugs his shoulders]

Now I have it in a bank down there in El Centro.

Do you want to see a book?

They just sent it to me, a big art book.

From Germany.

See, there is Salvation Mountain on the cover.

And inside there are five more pages of the mountain from different angles.

Full color.

The photographers—two of them from Germany—were here for three days.

Handsome book, Dewey.

Very nice presentation of the mountain.

Taschen—they're a well-known publisher.

Did they pay you?

No.

It don't matter.

I have all the money I need.

More than I ever had, because I was always real poor, you see.

I don't have a lot of expenses.

Except for my teeth.

I have this new set of teeth that I got done in El Centro.

What do you think?

They look good.

How do they feel?

They feel real good.

You have a new set of teeth and you've become a world-famous artist.

You don't mind that designation—artist?

At first when someone even mentioned me being an artist I'd correct 'em.

No, no, that ain't me.

But then it happened so often I got to feeling I should feel good about it.

Shoot, I don't care what people call it.

If they want to push the mountain as art, boy, I'm glad you like that artwork. [laughs]

Just so "God is Love" is up there and folks can come and draw their own conclusions.

What about apprentices?

There's so much interest in what you're doing, I'm sure you can get some young people to help you with the hoisting and heavy stuff.

That's true.

The heavy work is harder for me than it used to be.

Well, I did have a couple young fellows volunteer to help and they came from up there in Oregon all ready to do the heavy work.

Except one of the boys brought his mother with him.

She was a very religious lady, she took one look at the flowers I painted in all them colors and she scolded me.

She said: "You got to take them flowers down because you can't preach Jesus pretty."

"If you truly love Jesus," she said, "you are going to be persecuted and people gonna hate you."

Now that didn't hit me good.

Jesus is a beautiful spirit so I always thought it is right that I preach Jesus pretty.

So what I done after she scolded me is I started putting even more flowers on the mountain.

I guess I'm stubborner than a mule.

You tell me I can't so something, look out.

[laughs]

See, I'm such a loner it's almost embarrassing.

I don't know how to explain that really.

I love people, but I've been out here a lot of years and I hardly know anyone's last name.

I smile at them and thank them for bringing paint and groceries.

But when I get too close to folks, they sort of want me to do it their way.

And most of the time their way is right.

But I still like to do it my way.

I'm-a-gonna make lots of mistakes, but let me make them with God lookin' over me.

So you work alone.

But you and Salvation Mountain are all over the virtual world.

You have your own web site and blog, right?

Some young people from the LA area came up with the idea and I said fine, as long as they took care of it.

Which, I guess, they're doing.

I don't have a computer myself, but folks tell me it looks

real nice.

You're even on YouTube, videos of you constructing the mountain.

That's what they tell me.

It makes me happy to hear because not everyone can make it all the way to the Slabs to see the real thing.

Do you think that all the interest in Salvation Mountain has to do with a renewed faith in Jesus and the word of God?

Or does it have to do with the oddity of a person erecting a colorful mountain in a remote desert?

I don't rightly know.

I hope it's about Jesus, because without him the mountain wouldn't exist.

But it may not happen right away either, this true appreciation of Jesus.

As long as it happens sometime and Salvation Mountain is still standing.

You asked before about the donations.

Where the money goes.

About every dollar that's donated I put back in the mountain.

The more it expands, the more it needs to be kept up, you see.

How much larger is the mountain likely to get, Dewey?

Well, that depends on Jesus.

Weep

You wept several times in *Tango*. Were those real tears?

    Paul [the film's protagonist] *wept. The tears were real.*

Did you wear earplugs on the set?

    Only when other actors recited their lines.

Otherwise you'd be liable to weep?

    Maybe.

You're one of the very few macho male stars who weeps a lot. On and off the set.

    Any reason you can pinpoint?

    You pinpoint, I'll weep.

The preceding is a portion of an interview I conducted with Marlon Brando re *Last Tango in Paris* about a year before he died alone in a LA hospital.

    As a boy in Nebraska he wept when he lost his pet rabbit.

As an adult, he wept in the courtroom while defending his son Christian's murder of Cheyenne's abusive lover.

Cheyenne, who later killed herself, was Brando's daughter and Christian's half-sister.

Rabbits weep—or shriek—in agony.

Most humans don't know that, or care.

Brando stood in the freezing half-mile long queue to pay respects to 21-year-old Chicago Black Panther leader Fred Hampton murdered as he slept by Chicago police and the FBI.

Brando may have been the only non-Black in the queue.

Nobody acknowledged him.

When he saw Fred Hampton's shot-up body he wept uncontrollably.

There is a moronic "Tea Party" congresshuman with a faux-tan from a benighted state who weeps 79 and-a-half percent of the time he opens his mouth.

The rest of the time he drinks vodka (American brand) and makes cruel pronouncements.

The reptilian billionaire Rupert Murdoch wept after hackers uncovered his corporate empire's ongoing blackmail of politicos.

Retiring head coaches are obliged to weep.

Sports stars who attain landmarks (with or without the juice), weep.

Televangelists wearing strong cologne and diamond pinky rings weep while pleading for forgiveness.

The working-class child weeps after winning a spelling bee.

"Third World" mothers weep when their 12-year-old sons are shot to death for throwing stones at the tanks of colonizers.

There is now a weeping ring tone on elite smart phones.

The mothers and sons are brown and poor.

John Berger writes of the "despair without fear" that characterizes the West Bank under Israeli control.

Palestinians will weep with joyous despair at one of their martyr's actions.

It could be that you have to inhabit fear to weep in a certain way.

I am not sure I can define "certain way" satisfactorily.

Rosa Luxembourg was fearless; she didn't weep.

Virginia Woolf's fear was razor-sharp; she didn't weep.

Mahler inhabited fear; he composed *Kindertotenlieder*, Songs on the Death of Children, while his own child, Maria, was ill but alive.

When she actually died Mahler wept monster tears.

I am listening to him now. *Das Lied von der Erde*.

The earth was firm then.

Giacometti wept, but not his delusional comrade, painter of disheveled young girls in distress: Balthus.

Balthus's mother was the poet Rilke's mistress.

Rilke was too busy being charismatic to weep.

His specialty was consciousness.

Marcel Duchamp wept only when he masturbated.

Blended his semen with paint in those late obsessions.

In most accredited cultures, it is strictly the females who weep.

Islam is an exception. Islam isn't accredited.

Viewing media versions of innocent Muslims murdered we're to assume they are vermin.

Would you weep at rats in a junkyard shot for fun by drunken teens?

Drunken white teens.

Gandhi, practicing disinterest (not uninterest) aided the untouchables without weeping.

Jains don't weep; they squat naked and silent in their temples mouths and noses covered fanning away microbes.

Were I to be twice-born I'd be a Jain, I think.

Jain from another planet.

If I come back a third time I'll conceive a Franciscan cultural practice.

Animals get first dibs.

Pawprints not language.

Down with daily dental flossing.

I know a soul who weeps over road kill but jeers at the death of a CEO?

The globe is swaying, about to slip off its axis.

Like the revolution of the just, weeping has lost its purchase.

Every wall erected to keep creatures out is a wailing wall.

My charge is revival.

Transforming torment into a principle of conquest.

I propose a collective Weep-In.

Global.

Not excluding black Africa and Bangladesh and East Timor.

Not excluding the aged whom the electronic "revolution" has left behind.

I draw again from the estimable "wound dresser."

Weeping animals, plants and stones, "hand in hand," traverse the benighted globe, commencing in the west, swaying south, east, north.

Even as I walk hand-in-hand / hand-in-paw, weeping, I stand sad-eyed by the gravest, the worst-suffering.

I pass my hand over their heads.

They are impressive in their weeping.

Tormented, restless, they weep until bloody, fruitless wars are over.

Climate change acknowledged and addressed.

Dehumanizing post-capitalism hacked, disempowered.

The invisible colored poor made visible.

The twisted made sound.

Enslaving technology disappeared.

How long will all that take?

Revolutionary Brain

The world being insupportable, any deviation will have revolutionary potential.

—Bataille

It has emerged that the brains of three leading members of the violent revolutionary group, the Red Army Faction (RAF), including its co-founder, Andreas Baader, have disappeared after being preserved for **scientific research**.

The **grisly revelation** comes just days after the twin daughters of Ulrike Meinhof, the other RAF founder, finally won permission to have Meinhof's brain returned for burial.

Meinhof's brain was extracted after her alleged suicide in prison in 1976, but for years its whereabouts remained a mystery. Last month it was revealed that the brain had been **secretly preserved** in a Frankfurt laboratory.

The RAF, also known as the Baader-Meinhof Gang, began a campaign of political killings and kidnappings of senior business leaders in the early '70s aimed at overthrowing the German state which they called "**Nazi capitalism**."

Meinhof died of hanging in her cell in Stuttgart's Stammheim Prison on May 9, 1976; her comrades Baader, Ensslin and Raspe, were found dead in their cells in Stammheim Prison on "**Death Night**," October 18, 1977.

The Red Army Faction cell block had been touted as the most secure in the world; the press was filled with anecdotes of lawyers questioned and searched for an hour or more before being admitted to visit clients. When it was announced that Baader and Raspe had shot themselves with guns smuggled into their cells and that Ensslin had hanged herself, the reasonable assumption was that the **authorities assassinated** them as well as Meinhof the year before.

Their dead bodies were promptly autopsied and their brains extracted and given over **to Science.**

Josef Kohl, CEO of the Neurological Research Institute of Heidelberg University where initial tests were done, could not account for the disappearance of the brains. They might have been moved to make way for other organs and **finally burned**, he said, but he would not rule out theft.

Now the brain of Ulrike Meinhof has unexpectedly reappeared in the possession of a Frankfurt-based medical pathologist who insisted on anonymity. According to the pathologist, Meinhof's 1962 brain surgery in which a benign lesion was excised generated **her transformation** from a talented, ambitious journalist to co-founder and intellectual leader of the revolutionary Red Army Faction, which spread fear across West Germany in the '70s into the 1980s, after her death.

The anonymous pathologist told a news conference on Tuesday that he gained possession of the brain in 1997 after applying for permission to examine it. Previously it was held by a Stuttgart neurologist **named Muehl** who had conducted the autopsy after her "suicide."

The RAF carried out a campaign of killings and bombings against **leading industrial** figures, several of whom had been influential Nazis in the Third Reich.

The anonymous pathologist's involvement came to light last week when Meinhof's twin daughters in a lawsuit insisted that their mother's brain had been removed without the family's permission. Meinhof's daughters also filed a criminal complaint against the anonymous pathologist, accusing him of disturbing the peace of the dead. They are seeking to have the **brain buried** with their mother's remains in Berlin.

The latest revelations further suggest that the medical authorities had a **morbid fascination** with the revolutionary killers.

An unauthorized plaster death mask of Andreas Baader had evidently been made by one of the anonymous pathologist's medical team and he—or someone—had mixed his **own semen** with the plaster.

German authorities were said to be **conducting DNA** tests to uncover which of the anonymous pathologist's medical team's semen was involved in Baader's death mask.

Andreas Baader was a telegenic Brando-type bad boy who turned to political terrorism for the **methamphetamine-like rush** it gave.

The news of the plaster and semen death mask of Andreas Baader comes amid official concerns that a series of recent videos about the violent '70s have portrayed the terrorist killers as **pop icons**.

Celebrations of revolutionary violence unsettle German authorities **who claim** to be always on the lookout for a resurgence of Nazism.

Prosecutors are now examining documents from the time of Meinhof's death to establish how her brain came to be preserved for 30 years and whether **any offence** was committed.

**
Revolution Post-Mill

Electro Torment In The Funk Garage: 6 Bondage/BDSM WMVs

Teen Slut Swallowing Globs Of Hot Nut Butter: 4 Cumshots MPEGs

Blonde & Jap Swap Ass Cum: 3 Anal/Ass MPEGs

Pee Lovin Black Chick Begs For Mo': 4 Piss WMVs

Roughneck Mick Jacks His Dick: 6 Gay MPEGs

Mex Babe Spreads Pink Gets Meatstick: 3 Hardcore MPEGs

Thai Tight Twat Sucks Up Quart Sized Beer Bottle: 4 Fetish/ Bizarre MPEGs

I Love To Piss Myself Then Get Shagged: 4 Hardcore MPEGs

Bitch Fucks Up & Has To Bang Her Black Boss Monster Cock: 4 Interracial MPEGS

Thick Ebony Pissed & Boned: 3 Hardcore MPEGs

MILF In Pantyhose Gets Phat Ass Stuffed & Face Jizzed: 4 Mature Ladies WMVs

Big Mamma Wraps Her Boobs Round A Stiffy: 6 BBW WMVs

Shaved Head Babe Takes Cock For The Rock: 4 Hardcore MPEGs

Cougar Stalks Son's Pal & Plugs Him With Strapon: 5 Hardcore MPEGs

Hardcore Hot Wax Lesbo Threesome: 6 Bondage/BDSM WMVs

Dominatrix Drills Fem Slave's Snatch: 6 Bondage/BDSM WMVs

Texas Twins Dip Their Honeypots In Bubble Bath: 2 Young Ladies WMVs

Teen Babe Tossing Hunk's Salad: 3 Fetish/Bizarre MPEGs

Pornstar Sirena Sassy Slurps Every Last Drop Of Goo: 4 Cumshots MPEGs

Tiny Titted Blanca Takes Two Big Dicks In Pooper: 3 Anal/Ass MPEGs

Fisting Hard A Shaved Wet Puss: 4 Fetish/Bizarre WMVs

Slutty Granny Doing Herself With Batsized Dildo: 4 Mature Ladies WMVs

Twelve Surfer Dudes Jizz Trannys Face: 3 Blowjobs/Cumshots MPEGs

Cheating Wives Do It For $$$: 4 Amateur WMVs

Massive Black Cock Gives Pearl Necklace: 3 Big Dick MPEGs

Mature Brit Bitch Milks Rasta Cock: 3 Interracial MPEGs

Porn Chick Foursome Chain Pussy Licking: 4 Lesbian WMVs

Ivy League Coeds Fucking Sex Machines: 3 Young Ladies WMVs

Hot N Heavy Shemale Sex: 6 Trans WMVs

Two Muscle Bears Eat Each Other's Ass: 5 Gay MPEGs

Horny Hung Tranny Pleasures Two Studs: 4 Trans WMVs

Naive Emo Chick Giving Backseat Blowjob: 4 Blowjobs/ Cumshots MPEGs

Ebony Plump Rumps Humped By Black Horsedicks: 8 Big Dicks MPEGs

Innocent Game Of Truth Or Dare Turns Into Wild Orgy: 3 Amateur WMVs

Horny Fem Prof Deepthroats Frat Boy After Class: 4 Blowjobs MPEGs

Slut Tugs On Hard Cock Till She Gets Her Face Painted Jizz: 3 Amateur MPEGs

Kinky Shaved Chubber Whips Her Whip: 6 Big Tits WMVs

Long Tongued Cowboy Licks Grannys Snatch In Spooky Graveyard: 4 Hardcore MPEGs

Phat Butt MLF Boned Hard On Bar Stool: 6 Mature Ladies MPEGs

Tiny Asian Teens Smoke Huge Meat Cigars: 4 Interracial WMVs

Kinky Lesbo Powerplay: 6 Bondage/BDSM WMVs

Uh-Oh A Dominatrix Wearing Glasses With An 18 Inch Strap-On: 6 Bondage/BDSM WMVs

Chick In Chains Gets Her Snatch Snatched: 6 Fetish/Bizarre WMVs

3 Young Babes Play With Mud: 4 Young Ladies MPEGs

Superhung Tranny Porks Eager Boytoy: 6 Trans WMVs

Brunette & Redhead Trade Anal Creampie: 5 Anal/Ass MPEGs

Wifey With Huge Melons Facialized: 3 Big Tits WMVs

Skinny Goth Does Gloryhole In Raunchy Loo: 2 Blowjobs/Cumshots

Kristina Flashing Fake 32ddds In Convenience Store: 4 Big Tits WMVs

Real Amateur Housewife Home BJs: 4 Blowjobs/Cumshots WMVs

Korean Beaver Balling Big Dick: 9 Asian WMVs

Mature Lesbos Caught With Sextoy In Mens Toilet: 6 Lesbian MPEGs

Young Hottie Swallows Thick Cream Enema: 3 Teen MPEGs

Hunky Amateur Stroking: 5 Gay MPEGs

Hot Pigtail Pisses Boyfriend: 3 Hardcore MPEGs

White Boys Work Over Busty Nubian: 3 Interracial MPEGs

Two Dirty Moms Slobber Big Black Salami: 5 Mature Ladies MPEGs

Nice Nanny Gets Rammed In The Browneye: 5 Hardcore WMVs

Three College Gals Have Clit Lickin Fun: 3 Lesbian MPEGs

Gorgeous Ebony Gangbanged By Rednecks: 3 Interracial MPEGs

Tiny Little Ripe Rump Slathered In Cream: 3 Young Ladies MPEGs

Indian Chick Swallows Swamis creamy curry: 4 Asian WMVs

Twink & Bear In Raunchy Suck N Fuck: 6 Gay WMVs

Busty Pregnant Babe Gets Her Milk Pumped: 4 Fetish/Bizarre WMVs

Sluts Bound In Latex: 2 Bondage/BDSM WMVs

Sperm Spitting Bukkake Fetish Panic: 4 Asian WMVs

Wacko Bitch Uses Speculum To Climax: 5 Fetish/Bizarre WMVs

Euro MMFF Cumshot Extravaganza: 3 Group WMVs

Hot Brunette Gets Raunchy Rimjob: 3 Anal/Ass MPEGs

Mature Street Skank Plays Suck & Tell: 3 Hardcore WMVs

Hot Booty Blonde In 9-Inch Heels Boned Hard: 3 Anal/Ass MPEGs

Slave Slut Gets It In BDSM Dungeon: 6 Bondage/BDSM WMVs

Chubby Using Toes To Diddle Hard Cock To Cum: 4 BBW WMVs

Asian Housewife Squatting & Peeing: 4 Fetish/Bizarre WMVs

German Slut Ketchup Enema: 5 Fetish/Bizarre WMVs

Naughty Girl Spanked & Pissed: 4 Bondage/BDSM WMVs

Big Breasted Jane In Tittie Torments: 6 Bondage/BDSM WMVs

Spunktastic Cockgobblers Go Public In Strip Mall: 2 MPEGS

Fem Wrestler Gets Cameltoe Puss Licked: 6 Lesbian WMVs

High School Hotshot Bones Bubble Booty Cheerleader: 5 Hardcore WMVs

Petite Lisa Loves Black Ghetto Cock: 3 Interracial WMVs

Black Preggo Babe Squirting Chocolate Milk: 4 Amateur WMVs

Crazy voyeur Creaming On Sleeping Girl Boobs: 5 Voyeur MPEGs

Hentai Girl Rides Cock & Gets Facejizzed: 4 Anime MPEGs

Natasha In Bi-Action: 3 Pornstars MPEGs

Cute Redhead Jerks Sperm From A Cock: 4 Blowjobs/Cumshots MPEGs

Zitty Babe Rides The Sybian: 4 Amateur MPEGs

Skinny Chick Deepthroats Monster Dong: 3 Blowjobs/Cumshots MPEGs

Hairy Bus Driver Cops Sorority Snatch: 3 Young Ladies MPEGs

Naughty Blonde Licks Black Guys Ass: 4 Interracial MPEGs

Sissies Watch Wives With Big Cock Strangers: 3 Bondage/BDSM WMVs

Ass Worship Facesitting: 3 Fetish/Bizarre WMVs

Lady Sarah Ass-Smothering: 5 Bondage/BDSM WMVs

Sweet Teen Monalisa Nailed Doggiestyle: 4 Young Ladies MPEGs

Filipina Nurse In Homemade Hardcore: 4 Amateur MPEGs

Young Clit Chick Gets Double Dicked: 7 Anal/Ass WMVs

Blonde Mature In Hardcore Bi-Threesome: 4 Mature Ladies MPEGs

Cumaholic Babe Doing Deepthroat: 5 Fetish/Bizarre MPEGs

3 Jap Chicks Assboned & Creamed: 4 Group MPEGs

First Gay Experience: 4 Gay WMVs

Lola Swallows Priests Holy Cock: 3 Pornstars MPEGs

Moresome Facialing Cum Crazy Cutie: 4 Blowjobs/Cumshots WMVs

Muscle Brunette Ramrodding Off-Duty Cop With His Own Baton: 4 Fetish/Bizarre WMVs

Things to Do

After your bath, sit naked, cross-legged on the Navajo rug,
smell your imposed smell: *L'Heure Bleue*, by Guerlain: notes of
bergamot, carnation, heliotrope, & contemplate fated Austrian-
Jewish writer Joseph Roth's enunciation:

"The world worth living in is doomed.

The world that will follow deserves no decent inhabitants."

Harold Jaffe is the author of 20 volumes of fiction, "docufic-tion," novels and essays. His writings have been anthologized widely, translated into numerous languages, and the recipient of several awards. Jaffe is editor of *Fiction International* and Professor of Literature and Creative Writing at San Diego State University.

www.ingramcontent.com/pod-product-compliance
Lightning Source LLC
Chambersburg PA
CBHW050902180626
46814CB00007B/2849